THIS BOOK BELONGS TO:

_____

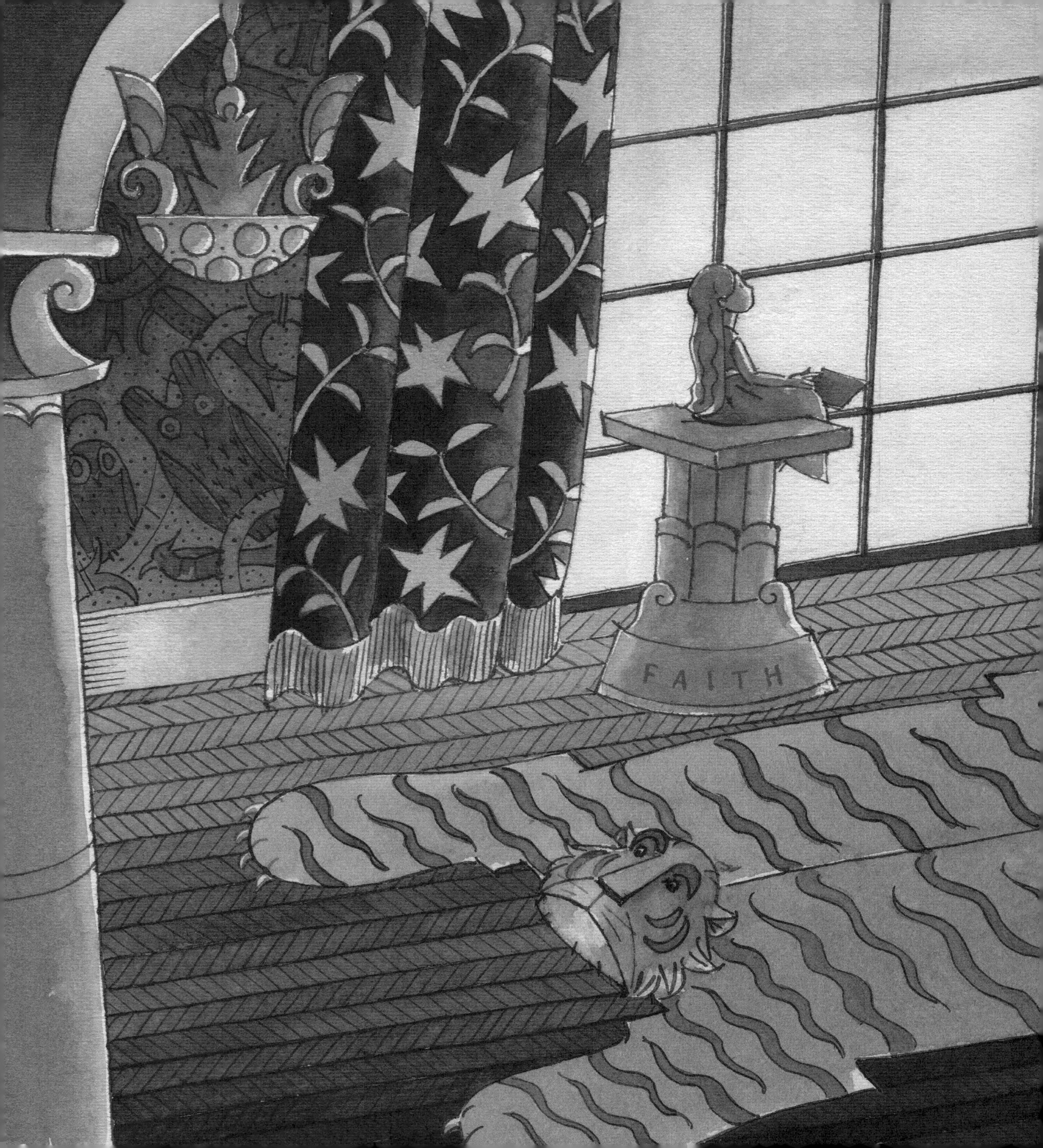
FAITH

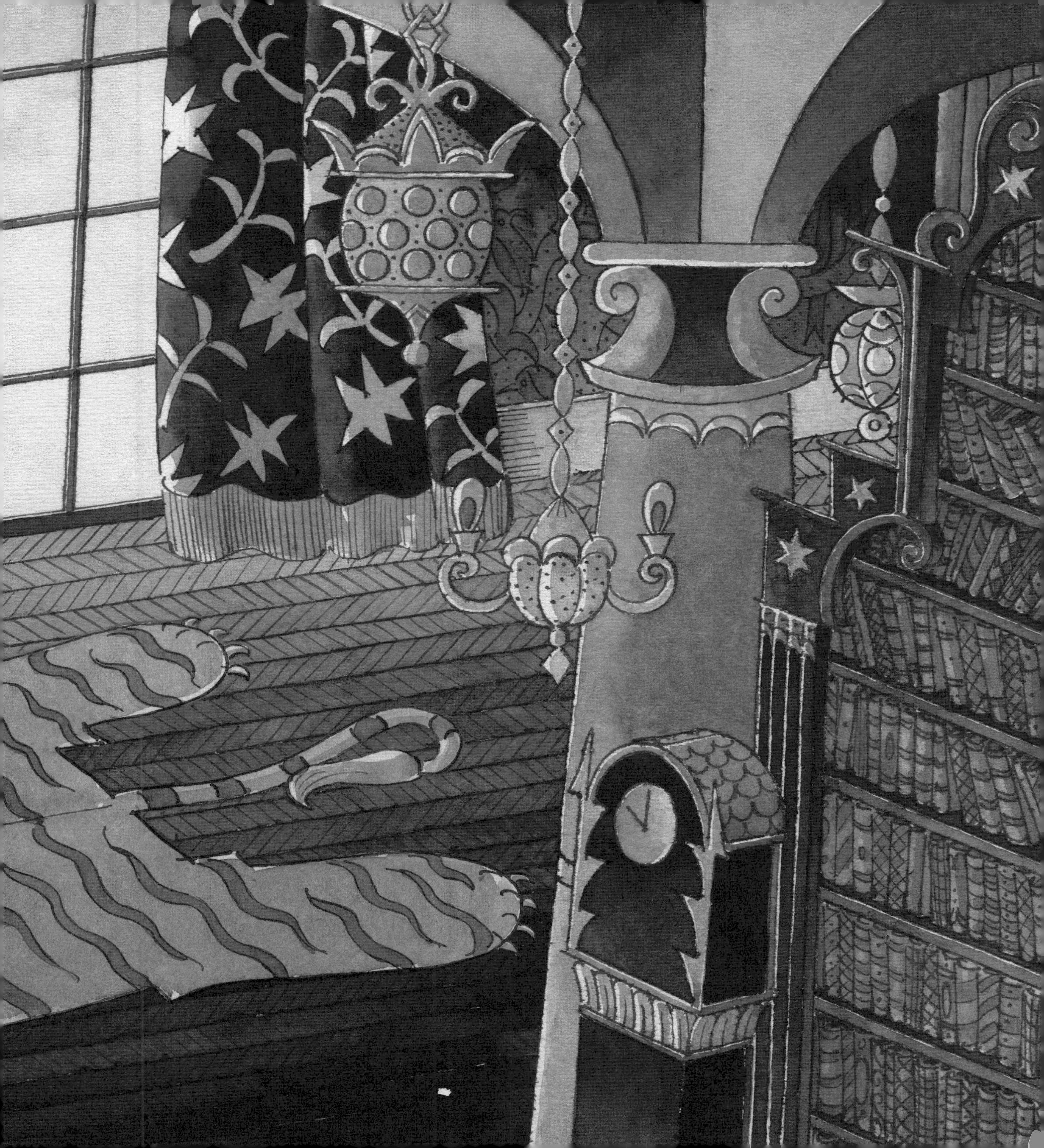

The Lying Carpet

this book is dedicated to Janice Thomson

Other books by David Lucas:

Cake Girl
Halibut Jackson
Nutmeg
Whale
The Robot and the Bluebird

First published in Great Britain in 2008 by Andersen Press Ltd.,
20 Vauxhall Bridge Road, London SW1V 2SA.
Published in Australia by Random House Australia Pty.,
Level 3, 100 Pacific Highway, North Sydney, NSW 2060.
Copyright © David Lucas, 2008.

10   9   8   7   6   5   4   3   2   1

British Library Cataloguing in Publication Data available.

ISBN 978 1 84270 441 7 (hardback)
ISBN 978 1 84939 017 0 (paperback)

The
Lying Carpet

David Lucas

ANDERSEN PRESS

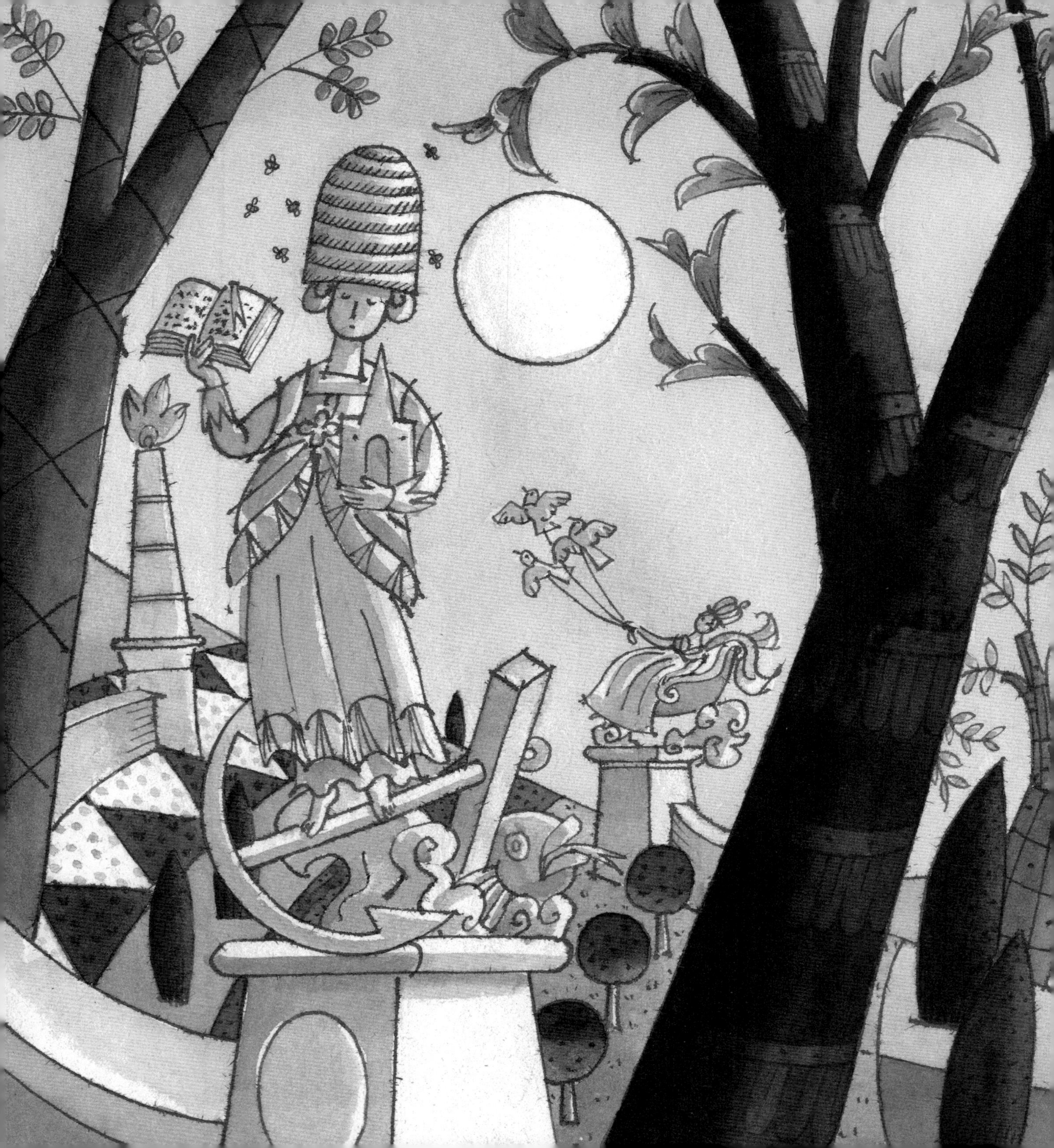

A Honeybee, fat with nectar,
knocked on the Window and said:
"The Truth is Bitter and Lies are Sweet,
but the Truth is better for you."

"That's all very well," said a Fly, trapped inside,
"but on this side of the glass, Truth and Lies are one."

Part One ✦

Faith had sat there for centuries, looking out of the Window,
looking up at the sky and the tall trees, and she had never said a word.

But that afternoon, as the light of the Sun moved across her face,
there was a glimmer of thinking in her eyes –
a tiny spark, a little thought that led to bigger thoughts.
She began to wonder where she was.
And how long she'd been sitting there.
"*Dear me*," she said, "I feel as if I've been asleep for ever."

"But you *have*," said a voice, a low voice, rich as fur and just close by.

She wanted to turn around.
But she couldn't move.

"I don't know what's the matter with me today," she said in a whisper.
She felt as if she were made of stone.

"It is a happy day!" said the voice. "You have spoken *at last*."

"Who's there?" said Faith. "Who are you?"

"I am a *carpet*," said the voice. "Down here, not far away. You might be able to see me out of the corner of your eye? Some of me, at least?"
Faith could see, on the very edge of her vision, a broad, striped shape on the floor.

"A *carpet*?" she said.

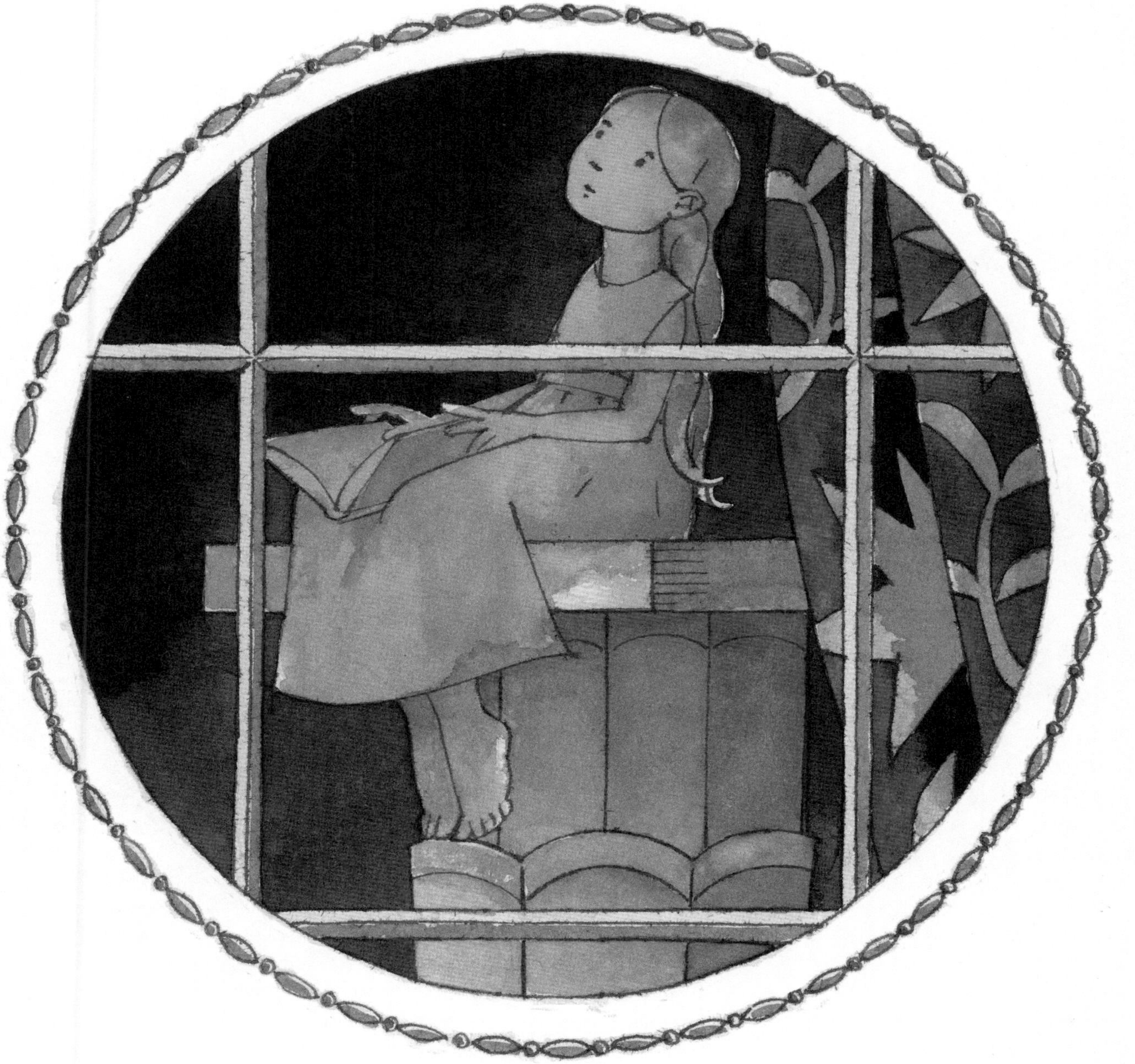

figure i: Faith

"A carpet," said the Carpet, "here to add a bit of warmth and colour
to what can sometimes seem such a gloomy room.
I like to think that I am both handsome and hardwearing –
but I have no illusions: I am *only* a carpet."

Faith was hardly listening.
"But what am I doing here?" she said.

"*Doing?*" said the Carpet.
And of course she couldn't *do* anything.

She wanted to rub her eyes.
She wanted to stretch and kick her feet.
But it was no good.
She couldn't even *blink*.

"You are a statue," said the Carpet,
"didn't you know?"

She *didn't* know.
"I have to *get up!*" she said.
But her body wouldn't budge.

"I can imagine it must all be a bit of a shock,"
said the Carpet.

FAITH

And he went on to explain, as patiently as he could,
that she was made of the finest marble,
going into some detail about violent geological processes
and the varieties of metamorphic rock,
before saying what an exceptionally *beautiful* statue she was.

"You are really very realistic," he said cheerfully.
"All finished off, with proper hands and feet
and a charming, innocent expression.
You might have been an urn or a pillar, or a step.
You are very lucky: you live in a fine house, with a lovely view,
and you have always been well looked after.
Some statues are chipped or broken, you know,
some are covered in moss and ivy."

"But what am I a statue *of?*" said Faith.

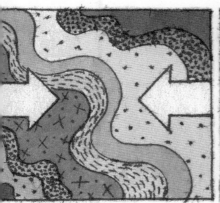

figure ii: violent geological processes

"A little girl," said the Carpet. "A little girl, with a book on your lap,
lifting your eyes to heaven.
Your name is *Faith*. F . . . A . . . I . . . T . . . H."

"But I thought I was *real*," she said, her voice quavering,
"I thought I'd just been here for a little while,
that I'd just sat down to look at a book."

"Of course," said the Carpet. "Why shouldn't you dream you're real?
You *are* astonishingly lifelike. The Painting has similar trouble.
It dreams it is a flock of sheep. I have heard it bleat."

figure iii: the Painting

"Then I'm stuck here *for ever*," she said, "just an ornament?"

The Carpet assured her that she was much more than that:
she was an important *work of art*,
and he went on to speak at some length about
the history of the figurative arts.

FAITH

figure iv: a history of the figurative arts

"You," he said, "are '*allegorical*', a representation of a great virtue. You come from a very good family."

"Do I?" said Faith.

"There was your grandmother, Prudence," said the Carpet,
"with two faces, talking to a snake.
Your mother, Fortitude, magnificent in a suit of armour,
an anvil on her head.
Your Aunt Temperance, poised on the sail of a windmill, on one leg,
sipping tea from a teacup and just about keeping her balance.
Cousin Liberty, winged and wearing leaves and dancing on a cloud.
Your Sister Charity, holding her own heart upon a plate,
and Hope, unfinished, barely begun, but all the more poignant for that.
Fine pieces of work, every one.
But you, Faith, you were best of all."

Faith had no memory of any of this odd family of hers.

"I suppose," said the Carpet, "it is unlikely that you ever spent very long all together in the same room."

FAITH

LIBERTY

FORTITUDE

HOPE

PRUDENCE

CHARITY

TEMPERANCE

figure v: a family of Virtues

"But you must remember being made?" he said.
"You must remember the noise – the banging and clanging and dust?
That first glimpse of the world as the Sculptor opened your eyes to the light?"

"I don't remember any of it at all!" said Faith, cross with herself.

On the outside of the window a snail climbed the glass, its eyes on stalks.

Faith sighed.
"How am I going to pass the time," she said,
"if I can't do anything? If I can't even read my book?"

The Carpet said that he had always found that talking
was the pleasantest way to pass the time.
"And I've always felt I could talk to you about anything," he said,
"whatever crossed my mind.
But now our conversation need not be so one-sided."

"Oh dear," said Faith, "you didn't think I was ignoring you, did you?
Sitting here with my nose in the air?"
"No, no," said the Carpet,
"I always liked to think what a good listener you were.
I'm often told I talk too much.
A good carpet should really only speak when absolutely necessary –
when the house is on fire, for example.
But I am not a *good* carpet."

FAITH

figure vi: the Sculptor at work

"I don't know if I can be a *good* statue," said Faith.

She watched as two butterflies
danced around one another
away up into the sky.

She was waiting for the Carpet to say something.

A fly circled noisily,
somewhere in the middle of the room.

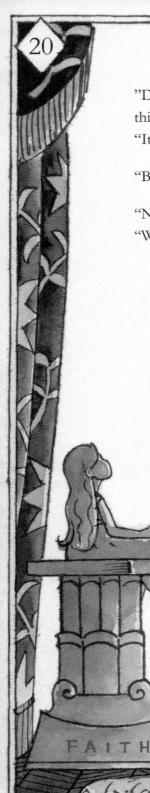

"Do you like being a carpet?" said Faith, at last,
thinking it was a good start to a conversation.
"It doesn't really matter if I like it or not," said the Carpet.

"But I'm sure you are a beautiful carpet," said Faith.

"Not everyone thinks so," said the Carpet. "Some people have had quite a fright."
"Who would be scared of a carpet?" said Faith.

"I am only a carpet," said the Carpet, "but I look like a tiger."
"A *tiger*?" said Faith.
"Yes, I am such a gentle, domesticated thing," said the Carpet,
"that it might surprise you to know that I was once *carnivorous*.
I killed to eat: lambs, piglets, calves, fawns,
even little children if I could catch them.
But have no fear. I'm quite harmless now.
I have been *civilized*.
Carpets have been known to drink blood,
but a carpet will drink spilled tea just as well,
which a tiger will not."

figure vii: the hunter

And then the Carpet said what sharp claws he had,
what white teeth, what glittering eyes, what bristling whiskers.
He claimed, at first, that his face was fixed in a smile,
then that, no, he was stuck mid-roar,
then he changed his mind again and said that
he was actually in the middle of an everlasting *yawn*.

Faith didn't know what to believe.

"But what do you *feel* like?" she said.

"I feel nothing at all," said the Carpet.
"Unless I'm trodden on, of course.
It might be better to say I *try* and feel nothing."

"You must feel something," said Faith.

"I just lie here looking at the skirting board,"
said the Carpet, "my mind as blank as a plank of wood."

"I don't believe you," said Faith.

"No," said the Carpet, "you're quite right. I'm lying."

And he began to speak about his simple life in the forest,
so long ago and what a happy animal he had been,
happy to breathe the clear air and play in the cool water
and roam wherever he liked.
He spoke about the pleasures of the companionship of his own kind –
of his beautiful tiger wife and his fine young cub who played between his paws
as they lay basking in the heat of the Sun.
"But what happened?" said Faith.

"I don't really like to talk about myself too much,"
said the Carpet abruptly,
and he changed the subject and lowered his voice,
as if he was telling her a great secret.
"You know, I *have* heard that you are not a statue at all.

FAITH

figure viii: the companionship of his own kind

I have heard that, in fact, you were once, long, long ago,
a perfectly ordinary little girl, but that you're under a *magic spell* —
that you were turned to stone."

"*Turned to stone*?" said Faith. "By who?"

Now the Carpet wasn't clear who might have put a spell on her,
or why, although he said that, so far as he knew,
it was in most cases the work of witches.
But then he said that perhaps it had just been an innocent mistake.

"*Perhaps*," he said, "you took an old, old book from a high, high shelf,
a book you had heard was dangerous,
a book you had been told not to touch.
How excited you were to think you might find spells to bake biscuits
or change the colour of your hair!
But the book fell open on a *dreaded* page and your eyes had only
to read the words and you were turned to stone.
There is, after all, a book open on your lap."

Now Faith was tingling with excitement.
A thrill ran through her. She *had* been real.
And she need not be stuck *for ever*.

"Spells can be *broken*!" she said. "Can't they?"
The Carpet said that, yes, they could.
"But *how*?" said Faith. "Do you know?"

figure ix: witches

FAITH

figure x: turned to stone

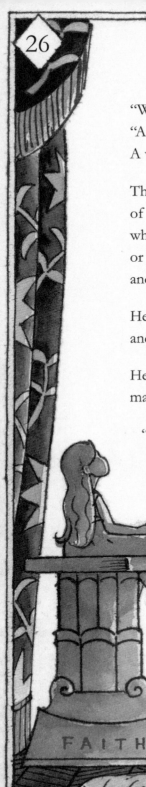

"Who can say for sure?" the Carpet replied.
"A wave of a wand? A kiss?
A word? Perhaps even a thought?"

Then the Carpet told her stories
of certain people he had heard of
who had been turned into trees or teapots,
or into swans or frogs or crickets,
and how each of them was at last freed from enchantment.

He told the story of a lady asleep for a hundred years
and woken with a kiss.

He told stories of how Magic Words had flung wide prison doors,
made mountains fly and parted the seas.

"I have heard," he said, "that it is often simply a matter
    of saying the *right* words in the *right* order at the *right* time."
        "Do you know any Magic Words?" said Faith.

            "*Abracadabra!*" said the Carpet, in his grandest voice.

                Faith sat in hopeful silence.
                Nothing happened.

                "Do you know any others?" she said.

FAITH

figure xi: a fairytale

"To be honest," said the Carpet, "nothing I have ever said
has had the slightest effect, for good or ill, on the world —
and I am an unusually talkative carpet with a wide vocabulary."

"But am I really under a spell," said Faith, impatient now,
"or just a statue? I want to know what's *true*!"

"I am in no position to know anything for sure," said the Carpet.
"My advice is that you should simply believe whatever you prefer."

And of course she preferred to think she was under a spell —
imagining she *did* have some faint memory of a former life,
and dreaming that one day the spell would be broken.
"I *feel* as if I'm under a spell," she said, "I'm *sure* I am."

figure xii: certain people he had heard of

Part Two

The Sun had dipped behind the trees
and the sky was the colour of gold.
Insects nosed amongst the ivy on the balcony.
A spider built her web.

Faith hadn't heard a sound
in the house all afternoon.
"Why is it so quiet?" she said in a whisper.
"Will anyone come and see me?"

"The Door is locked," the Carpet said.
"The Clock is stopped.
Dust gathers. No one comes."

figure xiii: the Maid

But then he explained that the Maid *used* to come once a week.
"She would wind the Clock,
clean the windows and sweep the floor,
bumping the broom against my face.
She always stopped to dust *you* carefully.
She liked to speak to you.
'Funny little thing!' she'd say, *'Still not finished your book?'*
And if it was sunny she'd say,
'What are you doing indoors on a day like this?'
She never spoke to me."

FAITH

"Did she know I was under a spell?" said Faith.
"Wasn't there something she could do?"

"I tried to tell her," said the Carpet, "but she wouldn't listen."
"But she will come again, won't she?" said Faith. "I can speak to her then."

"I don't know," said the Carpet.
"I don't know if she'll *ever* come again."

"But what's wrong?" said Faith.
"Why not? Has *everyone* been turned to stone?"

figure xiv: everyone turned to stone

The Carpet laughed – a kind of dusty snort of amusement.
"Oh, no," he said, "there are comings and goings now and then.
Lying here I am able to sense the tiniest vibration –
I sometimes hear footsteps, and hushed conversations.

figure xv: His Grace

"This was the favourite room of His Grace – his Library.
He always sat just *there*. That was his favourite chair.
But for months now he's been very ill,
confined to a bed in a downstairs room.
A cheerful room, I might add, and he is well looked after.
But he may never climb the stairs again . . ."

FAITH

figure xvi: the Housekeeper and the Nurse

The Carpet lowered his voice.

"You know, this morning I heard the Housekeeper and the Nurse, whispering to one another on the stairs.

They said that His Grace has been talking about *you* —

that he'd sat up straight, all of a sudden, to say that you were wide awake —

and that they must come and see.

They won't come, of course — they think he's just a mad old man —

but isn't it strange that this very day you chose to speak at last?"

"He must know about the magic spell!" said Faith. "Did *you* tell him?"

"Oh, no," the Carpet said, "*he* told me.

He had no time for the idea that you were a work of art —

although there is evidence that that *is* the truth."

"He told me that as a boy, he'd kissed you,
thinking you might come to life.
He was scolded for being so silly.
He tried everything to free you from enchantment.
He dabbled in witchcraft.
He performed elaborate rituals in the dead of night in exotic costume.
Nothing worked.

"He grew old and you stayed just the same.

figure xvii: the kiss

figure xviii: witchcraft

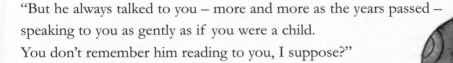

figure xix: reading

"But he always talked to you – more and more as the years passed –
speaking to you as gently as if you were a child.
You don't remember him reading to you, I suppose?"

And now Faith was sure she *did*,
that in her dreams she had heard stories and kind words
and felt someone close by.
"I'm *sure* I remember," she said.

"But it is so sad to think that he may never hear your voice,"
said the Carpet, "now that you have spoken at last.
Poor man! I couldn't help liking him:
a man who speaks to statues and carpets.
We would often talk late into the night,
as the fire burned low, his toes deep in my fur."

Then the Carpet's tone changed.
"But the truth is, we were not *always* friends.
The truth is, our relationship began *badly*.
In his youth His Grace travelled in the East
and tried his hand at hunting, as gentlemen did in those days.
It was *he* who fired the shot that stopped my heart.
I am a souvenir of his great foreign adventure."

Faith rang with shock.
She hadn't wanted to think about how the Carpet had ended up as he was.

And the Carpet, slowly, as if it caused him real distress,
began to tell her the story of that long-lamented day.

"I had gone out walking.
The forest had never looked more beautiful,
and without thinking I went a little further than usual.

"I smelled smoke on the breeze.
Flocks of birds flew up in alarm.
Suddenly, all around me the forest was aflame
and gangs of men, hollering and shrieking,
waving clubs and jabbing spears,
drove me into the path of a hunting party.

FAITH

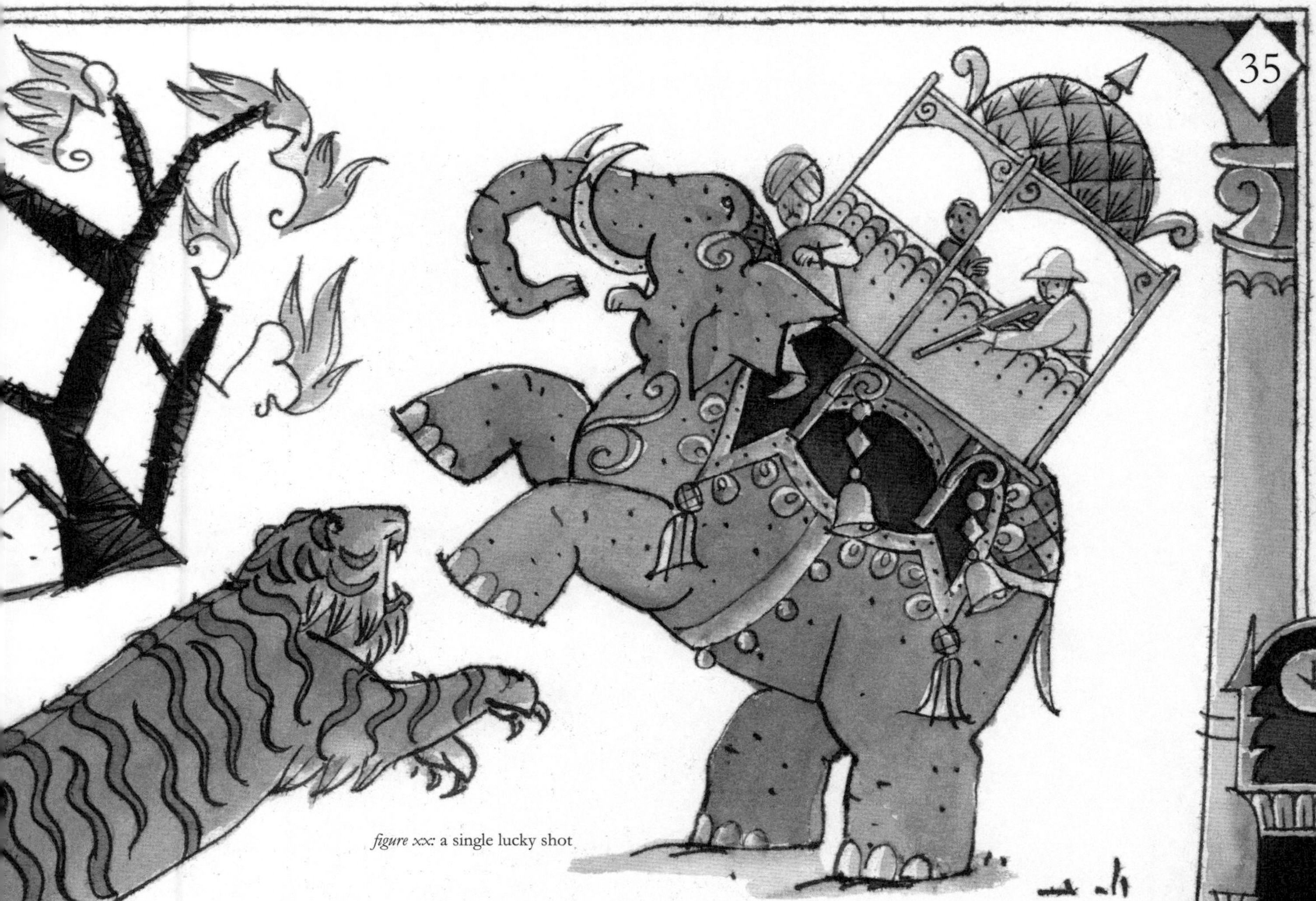

figure xx: a single lucky shot

"High on an elephant sat a man with a gun,
his face red, his eyes wide, his hands shaking.
I burst from the trees, in fury.

"I saw him hurry to steady himself,
the gun slipping in his hands.
With a roar, I hurled myself at him.
He *fired* – a single lucky shot.

figure xxi: (silence)

FAITH

"I was strung from a tree . . ."
The Carpet paused.

"How can I speak about what followed?
I was changed, that's all.
When at last my head was stuffed with straw and sawdust,
when glass baubles were sewn where my eyes had been,
I saw what I'd become: *a carpet*.

"I, who was stronger than the buffalo, quicker than the deer,
braver than the cobra, wiser than the stork,
the proudest of all God's creatures,
here I lie, *flattened*: a carpet, a hearth rug, a doormat,
with nothing to do but mourn the loss of everything I held dear –
my family, my freedom, my dignity."

Faith didn't dare to speak.
Now she understood why the Carpet might not want to dwell on the truth.

"Of course," said the Carpet,
"I often asked His Grace how he could have been so cruel.
He would just smile and say that I was making it up.
He said that I was a *fake*.

"He told me I'd been made in a factory, out of artificial fibres,
identical to dozens of others, and made *badly*.
He said that I was no more than a cheap joke of a thing.
He tugged my label to prove his point."

"But you can't tell me two *different* things!" said Faith. "Opposite things!
Anyway, I wouldn't like to think that either was true."

"We argued about it," said the Carpet.
"I said I could be *whatever* I wanted to be.
That I could even be two things at once if I wanted.
He just laughed.
So then I said that whatever the truth was I forgave him.

"I may be a fake.
I may have been a tiger.
I may be just the ghost of a tiger
here to haunt the house of the man who shot me.
I prefer to think that they are *all* true at once."

FAITH

figure xxii: fakes

"But they can't *all* be true at once," said Faith, bewildered.
"*Can't they*?" said the Carpet.

And now there was something in the Carpet's voice
that made her think that he wasn't just teasing her,
and that there was something more mysterious going on.

Part Three ❧

The Sun set, and the Room disappeared in shadow,
and as Faith sat in darkness, she was glad to hear
the comforting purr of the Carpet's voice, close by her side.
He told her stories of the other things that shared the room.
He told her the story of the couch, who was mad,
of the chair, so loyal to His Grace and now so sad,
of the wallpaper, whose dense pattern of birds,
the Carpet said, every now and then took flight,
making a great noise, and filling the air,
before settling again in silence,
in a different arrangement altogether.

figure xxiii: the wallpaper pattern in fli

FAITH

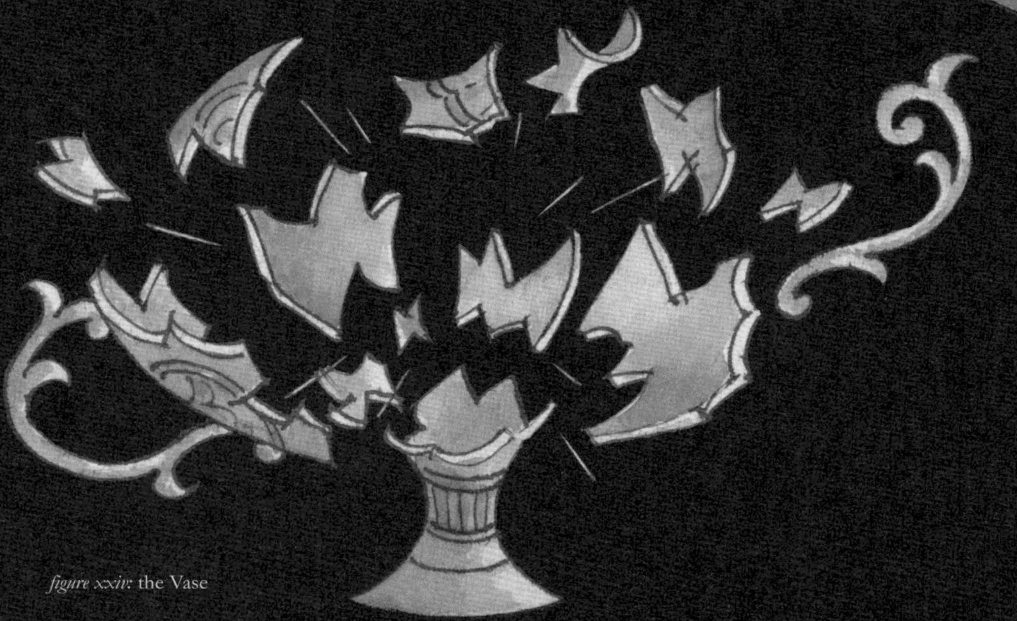

figure xxiv: the Vase

He said that there had been a beautiful Vase
stood there beside the Clock,
and that the Vase and Clock had loved one another.

But the day the Clock stopped,
the Vase had died of a broken heart,
and exploded with a noise like a gunshot,
showering the Carpet with fragments.
"Perhaps you heard something then," said the Carpet,
"perhaps you remember the Maid's surprise
when she found the Vase in pieces?
You might remember her sweeping up the bits?"

Faith did not.

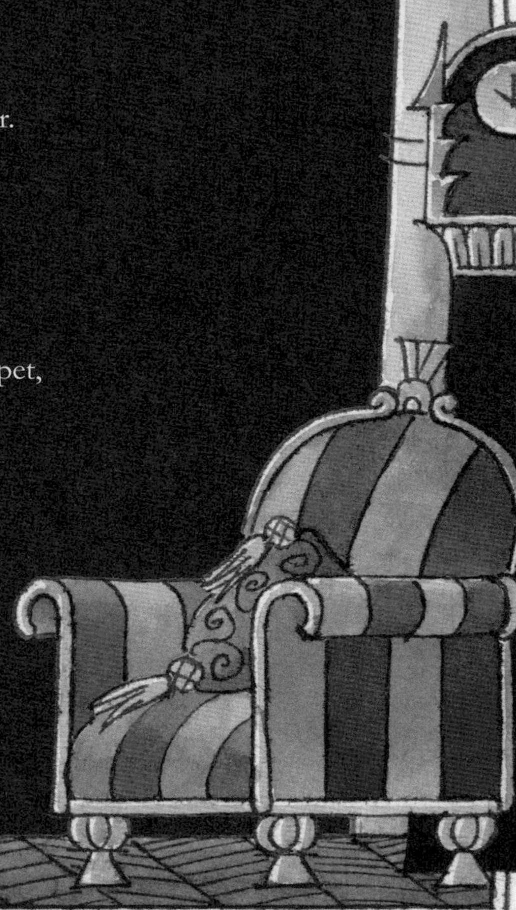

The Carpet was in the middle of a story about the Desk,
and the strange effect it had on anyone who sat down at it to write,
when he seemed to lose his way, and finally fell silent.
There was no response to Faith's repeated questions.

He was asleep.
And she was alone.
A lonely little girl turned to stone,
and pale as a ghost,
whispering to herself in the darkness.

And she began to feel afraid.
What if nobody came at all?
What if the old man died
and the house stood empty
and she was forgotten –
a little voice behind a locked door,
with only the Carpet for company?

FAITH

What if she was stuck just as she was, for a hundred years –
the house a crumbling ruin, the roof falling in around her,
the garden thick with weeds and thorns,
and the Carpet mouldering away, saying less and less,
until she was all alone, lost in a tangle of ivy and spiderweb?

And what if it was just too much to bear?

"What will I do *then*?" she said.
"Would I break if I screamed and screamed?
Would I shatter like the Vase?
Would the bits of me still think and feel?
A hand and a foot and a face arranged in a row,
and more unhappy than ever."

figure xxv: Faith, in pieces

But there above was a single star – burning quiet and bright.
And it seemed to Faith as if it was a kindly spirit looking down,
watching over her,
there to tell her that she wouldn't be forgotten,
and that one day, some day, the spell would be broken.

She was sure it was true.
Someone would find her and say the words that would set her free.
And thinking that one bright thought
she *could* be quiet inside, and not so afraid.
She could wait, patient as a rock,
while the dark hours passed.

FAITH

figure xxvi: the view from the window

Part Four

And now a new day was beginning at last.
A grey heron steadily crossed the sky.
In the distance a dog was barking.
The trees were full of singing birds,
and insects began to stir, zig-zagging in the warming air.

"*Wake up!*" said Faith.
The Carpet said nothing.
"Talk to me!" said Faith.

"I am *only* a Carpet," he said,
"I am not good company."
"But Carpet, please . . ." said Faith.

"My mind is a richly furnished mansion," said the Carpet,
"a mansion of many rooms,
but my thoughts have not yet come down to breakfast."

A thrush cracked snails' shells on the balcony.

"*Please*, Carpet," said Faith, "can't you tell me a story?"

figure *xxvii:* flooring

"I am only a carpet," he said, "I have seen so little of the world."
Then he paused, before saying:
"But I am an expert on the subject of flooring."

Faith sighed.

"I," said the Carpet, "am an authority on the habits of beetles . . .

figure *xxviii:* courtship

"The life-cycle of the Two-spotted Fur Beetle
has been a subject of particular interest to me . . .

figure *xxix:* the larval form of the Two-spotted Fur Beetle (enlarged)

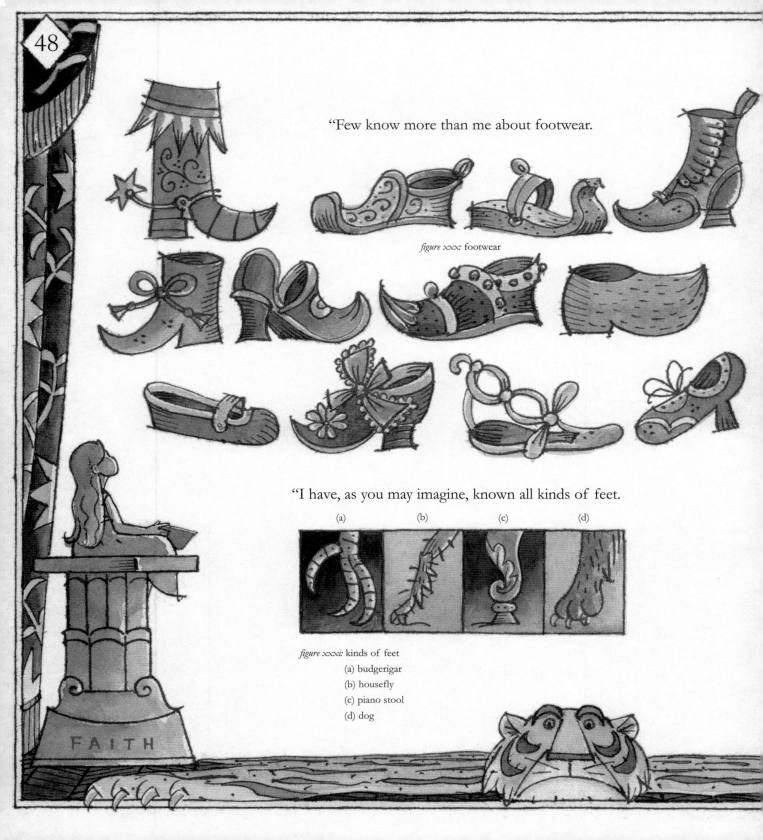

"Few know more than me about footwear.

figure xxx: footwear

"I have, as you may imagine, known all kinds of feet.

(a)   (b)   (c)   (d)

figure xxxi: kinds of feet

    (a) budgerigar

    (b) housefly

    (c) piano stool

    (d) dog

FAITH

"The prettiest foot I ever saw," said the Carpet,
"was the left foot of a dancing girl.
Before I knew what I was doing I'd declared my love.
She, the foot I mean, said that she loved me too,
that she'd never seen such a handsome carpet,
and that she wished we could be together always.

"But our happiness wasn't to last.

"The right foot was jealous
and kicked me hard,
and then the left foot whispered sadly
that she had to leave for the right foot wanted to go.

"I never saw her again."

figure xxxii: a pretty foot

"How could you love a foot?" said Faith.
"It was a silly infatuation," said the Carpet, "of which I am now ashamed."

"Tell me a proper story," said Faith, "a story with a happy ending."
And as the Sun moved across the sky, the Carpet told a long, long story,
a story about a *walking* statue and a *flying* carpet.

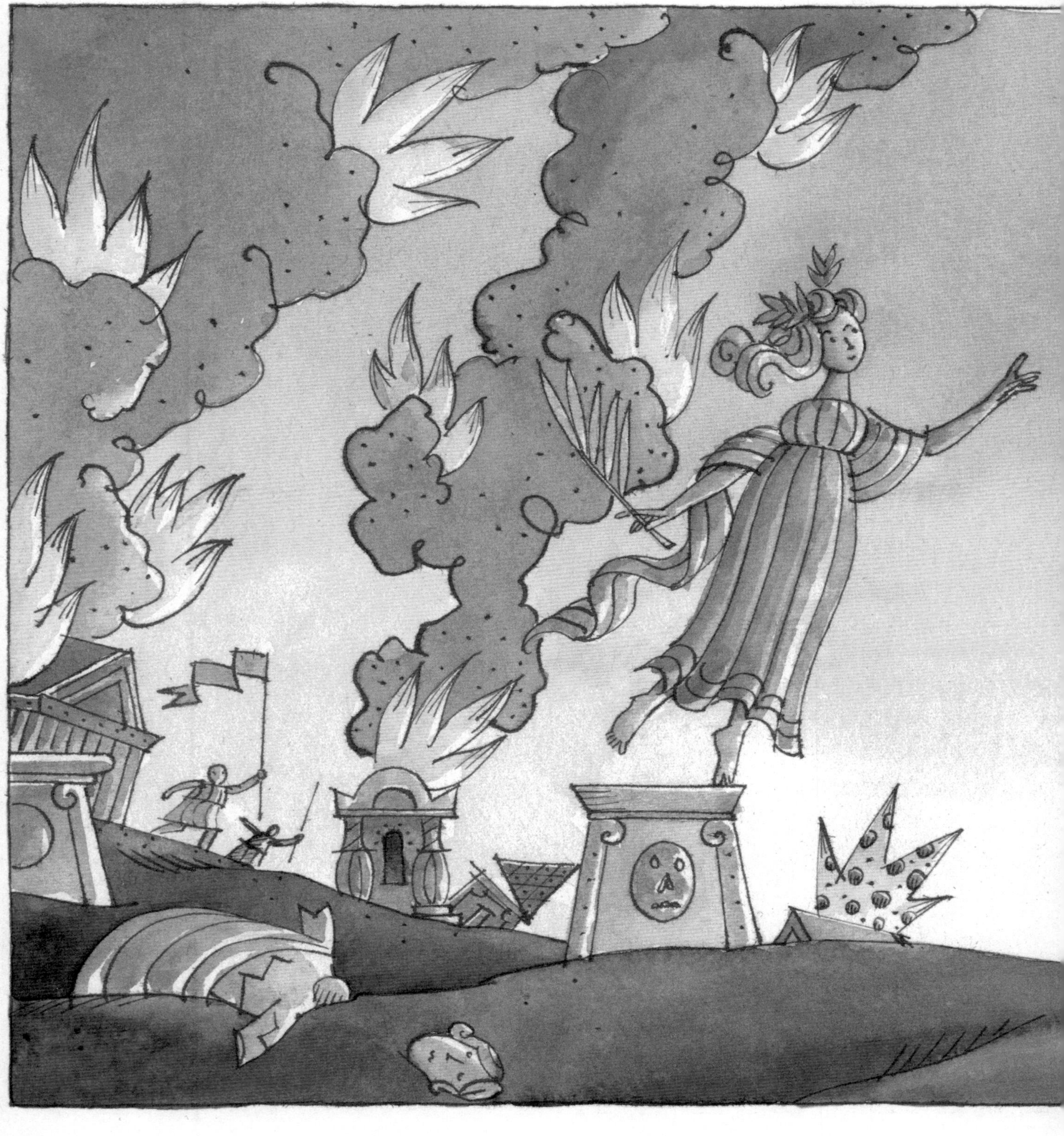

figure xxxiii: a walking statue and a flying carpet

Part Five

"Don't you wish *you* were a Flying Carpet?" said Faith,
when the Carpet had come to the end of his story.

"I don't waste time *wishing* for things," said the Carpet.
"I have a job to do – lying *here*."

"But you must think about all the long time ahead of us?" she said.
"About what's going to happen?"

"No," said the Carpet, "I don't. I am a carpet.
Do you think my life is a fairytale? With a happy ending?
No. My life is *flat*: without fear or hope.
I live entirely in the Present Moment –
without a thought for the Future or the Past."

Then he paused before saying:
"Some people say Time is a line – like a long piece of string.
For me it is a *Tangled Knot*."

Faith didn't know what he was talking about.
"I just want to believe things can change!" she said.

FAITH

She could see someone working in the garden,
clipping a little tree into the form of a bird.
She tried to call out. She tried to shout.
"I'm under a spell! Turned to stone!
Look! Up here! *Please.*"

But she could only speak in whispers.

She listened to the clip-clip
of the Gardener's shears
as he moved on and out of sight.

It was late afternoon now,
and the shadows were deep and long.
In the room a fly flew lazily this way and that.

"Little fly!" said Faith,
"I wish I could do as I please, like you."
The fly flew on.

figure xxxiv: the Gardener

"A fly is no more free than you or me," said the Carpet.
"It all depends on how you look at things . . ."
Faith interrupted him.
"But I always face the same way," she said sadly, "looking at the same bit of sky."
Then more brightly, she said:
"But you must have been moved about? Haven't you?
And been in different places and seen different things?"

The Carpet sighed.

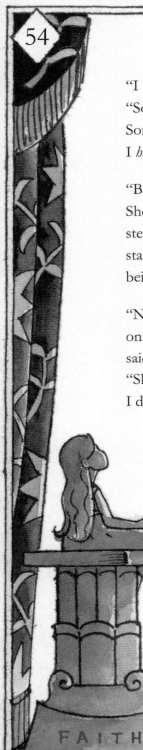

"I *have* been moved about," he said.
"Sometimes I'm rumpled and not quite flat and straight.
Sometimes I've been laid out the other way round, facing the other wall.
I *have*, in fact, been Outside. I have seen over the balcony."

"But what was it *like*?" said Faith.
She imagined throwing the windows wide,
stepping outside to breathe the sweet air,
standing with her arms outstretched,
being able to shout and dance and sing.

"Now and then the Maid would bundle me out
onto the balcony and beat me,"
said the Carpet gloomily.
"She would wallop me with all her strength.
I did not enjoy it.

"Yes, I've been Outside.
Yes, I've seen over the balcony.
Was my life improved?
Am I a *better* carpet for having suffered?
No. I see no virtue in upheaval.
Happiness is not to be found in *moving about*.
I am happy just as I am, thank you."

Faith was dismayed.
"But how *can* you be happy as you are?" she said.

FAITH

figure xxxv: the Carpet, beaten

"I enjoy the little things," said the Carpet, "the warmth of the Sun,
the pleasure of an Unscratchable Itch,
the tickle of an insect's feathery antenna.
I watch dust circulate in the air.
I watch it settle on my nose.

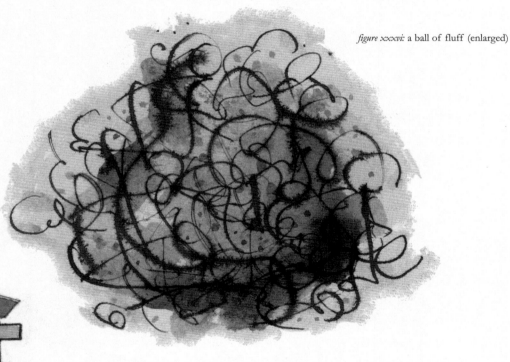

figure xxxvi: a ball of fluff (enlarged)

"*Sometimes* I see a spider or beetle emerge
from the gap between the skirting board and the floor.
Now and then a ball of fluff rolls by."

FAITH

And he went on to remind Faith how lucky she was
in comparison to his own less elevated circumstances.
"You *do* have a lovely view," he said, "there is always something to see.
The leaves will soon be turning red and gold.
Autumn is when the garden is most beautiful of all."

"But it isn't enough!" said Faith, "Carpet, what will I do?
I don't think I can bear being still much longer.
I'll break in pieces! I'm sure I will."

"You know," said the Carpet gently,
"I haven't really been telling the truth at all."

"But why do you lie to me?" said Faith.

"I lie because the truth is so hard to believe," said the Carpet.

"I don't *wish* I was a Flying Carpet.
I *am* a Flying Carpet.
I can fly away whenever I choose.

figure xxxvii: deserts, mountains, cities

"Of course I've been Outside –
I've flown away over the garden wall,
high in the sky, up above the clouds.
I have seen deserts, mountains, cities!"

It *was* too hard to believe.

FAITH

figure xxxviii: the Carpet, flying

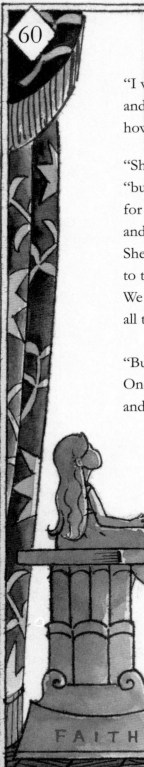

"I was taught to fly by a beautiful Persian Rug," he said,
and he told the story of his love for the Persian Rug –
how they first met when they were thrown together.

"She couldn't speak," said the Carpet,
"but I was sure she heard everything I said,
for one night she levitated, hovering for a moment,
and we took flight – away over the rooftops, under the stars.
She carried me along until I had the confidence
to try flying by her side, holding on only with an outstretched paw.
We swooped in and out of the clouds, tumbling through the air,
all the world laid out beneath us.

"But disaster struck one beautiful evening.
One of her stitches snagged on my claw
and she unravelled before my eyes.

"I was left trailing a long, silken thread,
flying on alone, over the desert, under the Moon."

And Faith wondered if the Carpet *had* once loved a rug –
perhaps really loved her – and now, staring at the skirting board, and alone,
he passed the time inventing stories –
telling himself she wasn't just *any* rug,
and that he was no *ordinary* carpet.

FAITH

figure xxxix: the Persian Rug, a romance

"Yes, she taught me to fly," said the Carpet,
"but I discovered the trick of Time Travel alone:
the trick of travelling without moving,
of moving up and down the floors of History like an elevator.
Of course you see me here now,
but I am often actually far off in the Future.
I holiday for weeks at a time in the Long Long Ago."

And then the Carpet claimed he was actually flying *all the time*,
in some other *Where* or *When*,
and that he was able to be in several places at once:
that he was telling a different story to someone else
in another room, at that very moment.
That room, he said, had a wonderful roaring fire,
and he could feel the glow of warmth on his face.

figure xxxxii: someone else in another room

FAITH

figure xxxxx: the Future

figure xxxxxi: the Long Long Ago

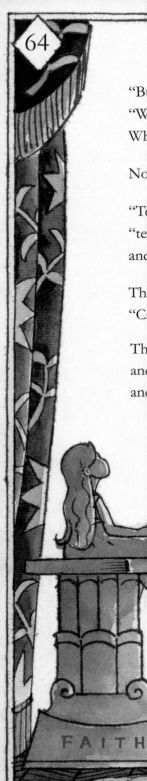

"But what about *us*, in *this* room?" said Faith.
"What will happen to us? Do you know?
What will happen when the old man dies?"

Now the Sun was setting and the sky was red as blood and fire.

"Tell me we won't be forgotten," she said,
"tell me the door will be opened and someone will find me
and hear me and believe that I'm under a spell."

The Carpet didn't reply.
"Carpet, *please*!" said Faith.

There were voices on the stairs,
and outside, she heard horses' hooves on the gravel path
and the sound of a carriage.

Suddenly the Carpet spoke.
"I'd seen it written in dust! In letters in the air!
I'd seen it spelled out in the flight of a moth and the footsteps of a beetle!"
"What are you talking about?" said Faith.

"That he would die the day you woke," said the Carpet.
"My friend, His Grace, is dead."

Faith shuddered.

"But yesterday . . ." she began and stopped.
She didn't understand.
"But Carpet is *any* of it true?" she said. "I don't know what to believe."

The Carpet said nothing.

FAITH

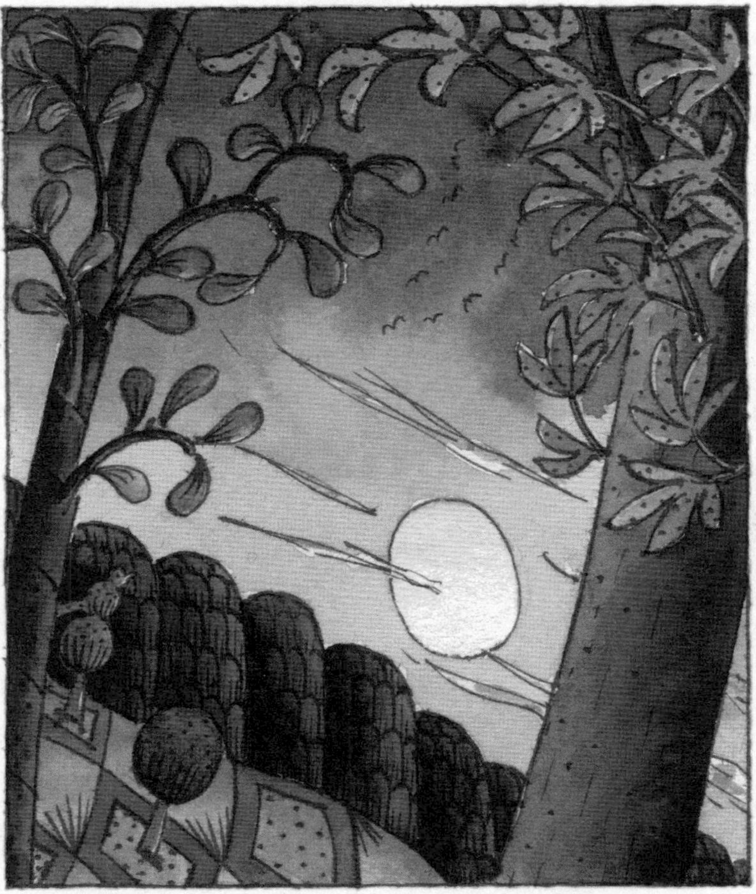

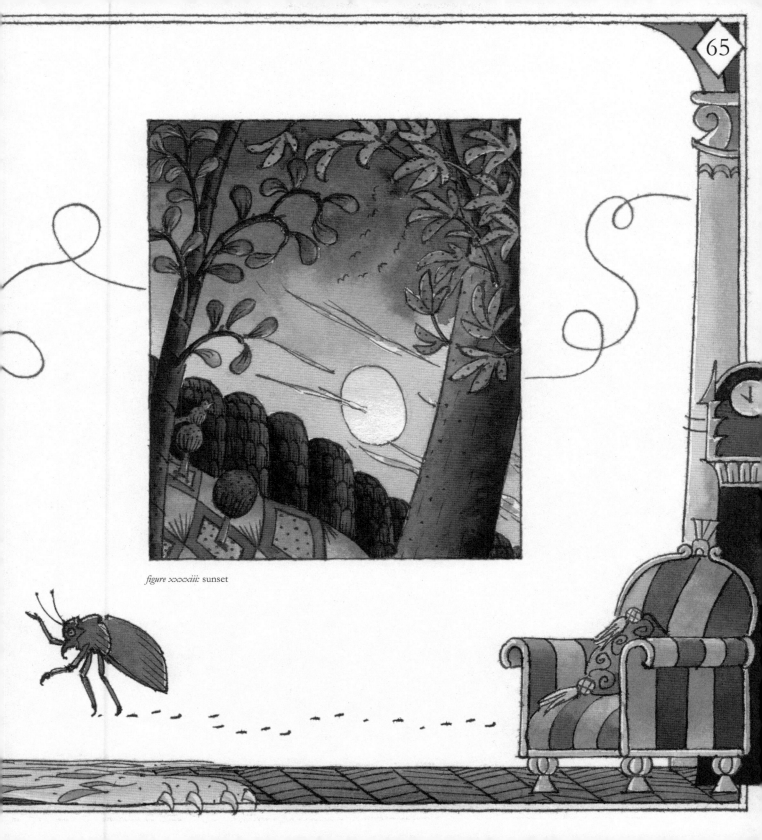

figure xxxxiii: sunset

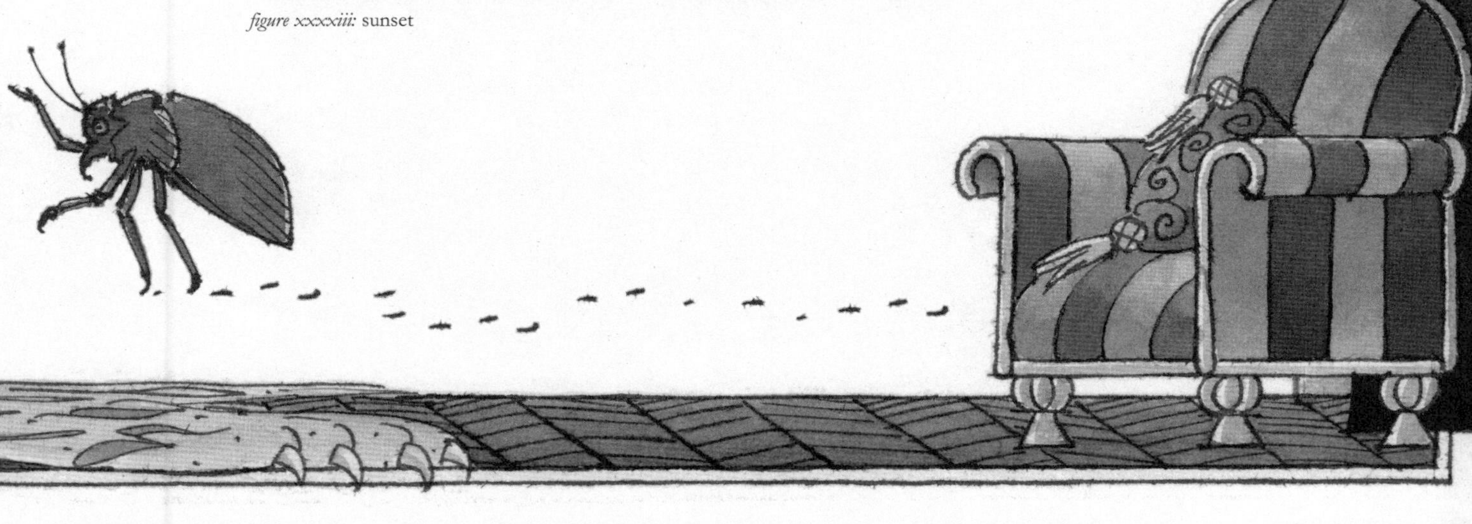

It was dark when suddenly the Carpet said, in a whisper:
"*Your Grace?* The ghost of His Grace!
I felt his slippers on my back.
He's sitting in the chair."

"You're frightening me," said Faith.
She was tingling with alarm.
In the dark, and unable to turn her head,
it was easy to imagine a presence hovering just out of sight.
But she could see the chair out of the corner of her eye.

"There's nothing there!" she said.

"He's gone," said the Carpet. "He only wanted to say goodbye.
He had a message – a message for you.
He said: *'Don't believe a word the Carpet says –
nothing he has said is true'.*"

Faith felt a flash of anger.
A tremor shot through her.
"Stop it, Carpet," she said.

FAITH

figure xxxxiv: slippers

"Of course," said the Carpet, "there is a chance I was seeing things.
It may have been a trick of the light,
or some kind of electromagnetic phenomenon.
The influence of the full moon on the impressionable mind
is well known to science."

figure xxxxv: the ghost

"But whatever it was," said the Carpet,
"whether or not I was hearing things, the voice spoke the truth.
Everything I have said is a *lie*. Nothing I have said is *true*."

Faith felt ready to erupt with frustration.
Her heart was boiling and molten:
"How can *nothing* you've said be true?" she said.

"I've been lying all the time," said the Carpet,
"I'm a *lying* carpet, not a *flying* carpet.
I said that you were turned to stone by magic.
I made it up.
I didn't expect you to believe me.
I've made it all up. His Grace. Ghosts. Everything.
Of course I didn't see a ghost.
I don't believe in ghosts.
But then, I can't see *you* either.
Why should I believe in you?
I'm sure I've just been hearing things.
I don't think you're *really* real at all."

"*No*," said Faith. "No, no, no! I *am* real. You *know* I am."

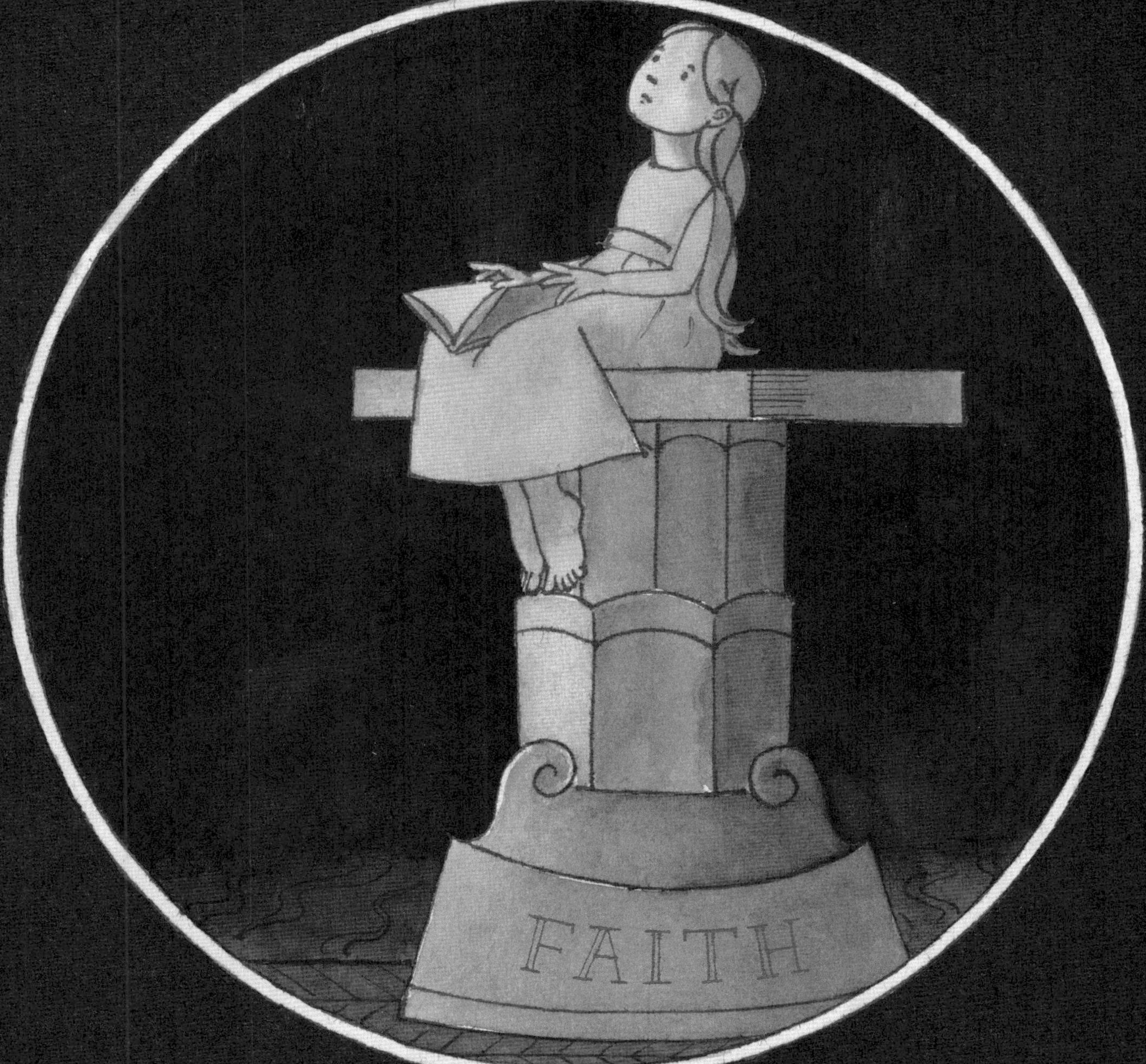
FAITH

figure xxxxvi: Faith

figure xxxxvii: she jumped to the floor

FAITH

And as she spoke her lip was trembling.
She suddenly noticed she'd clenched her fists.
Her face was hot and flushed with colour.
She kicked out with her feet, the open book slipped from her lap,
and she jumped to the floor.
She landed as soft as a cat.

The Carpet smiled.

She wasn't made of stone.
She was flesh and blood – an ordinary little girl, barefoot and laughing.
"The spell is broken," she said, "I don't know how."
"It was just the *right* words in the *right* order at the *right* time," said the Carpet.

She turned and saw the plinth – her name cut there in capital letters –
and there was the book – still plainly made of stone, but shut.
The Carpet felt her little feet in his fur.
She skipped across him and then, kneeling, gently stroked his face.

There was the trace of a wound above his eye.
"You are a tiger," she said.
"No," said the Carpet. "I *was* a tiger."
"And I *was* a statue, wasn't I?" said Faith.
"Yes," said the Carpet softly.

And she knew that he *had* seen the future.

"Then perhaps you *can* fly?" she whispered.

"I've been flying all the time," said the Carpet. "*Look.*"

Faith gasped,
her tiny hands gripped his fur –
the walls had vanished,
the wind was in her face,
her hair was streaming behind her,
they were high in the air,
flying through the night . . .

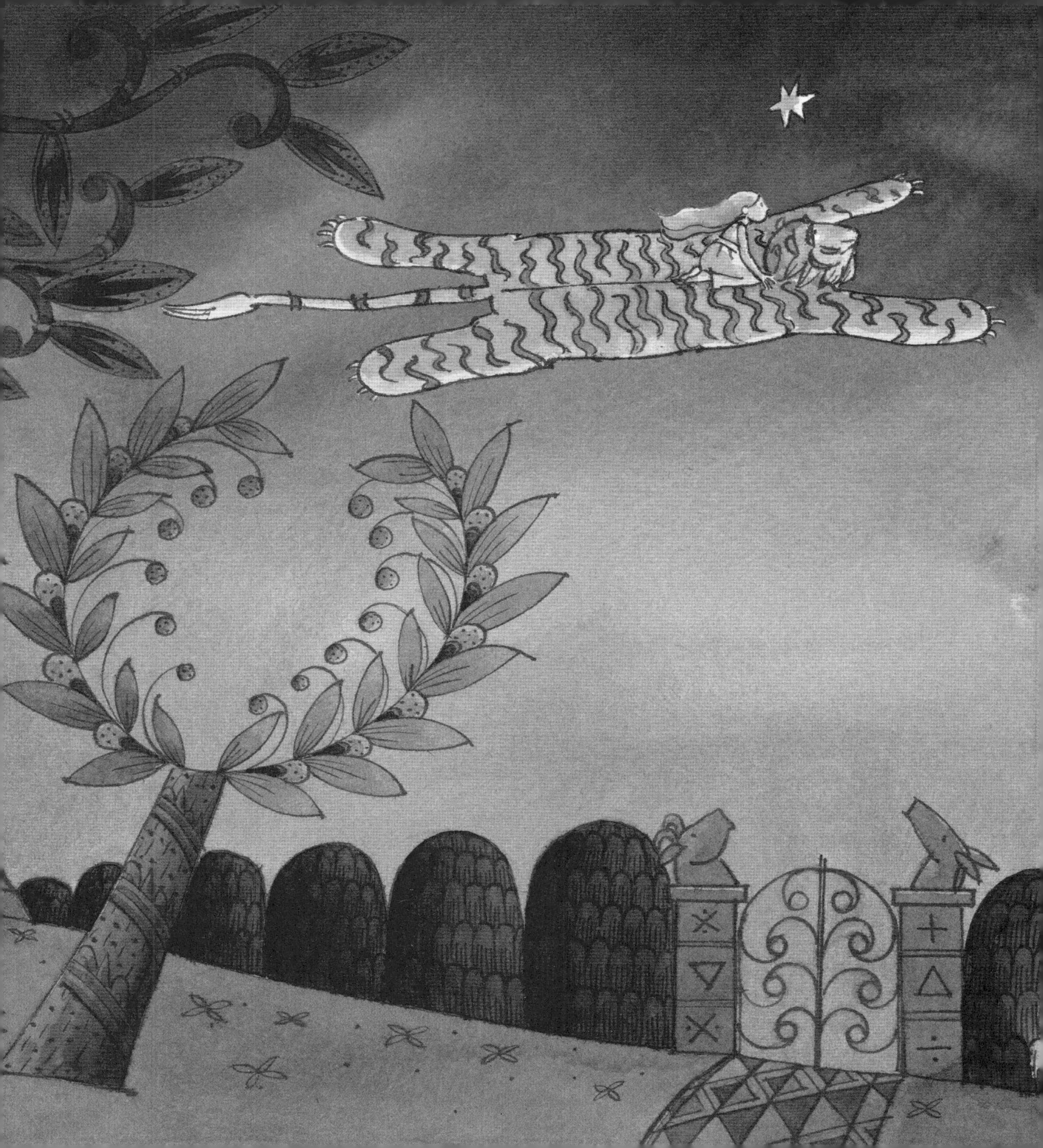

Epilogue ∽

There had been a house of course —
the home of a lonely old man,
who had seemed, to those who knew him,
much too fond of talking to himself.

figure xxxxviii: the shut stone book

And when, some days after he died,
the door to the Library was opened,
the Housekeeper shrieked to see the empty plinth,
the shut stone book,
and the space where the Carpet had been.

FAITH

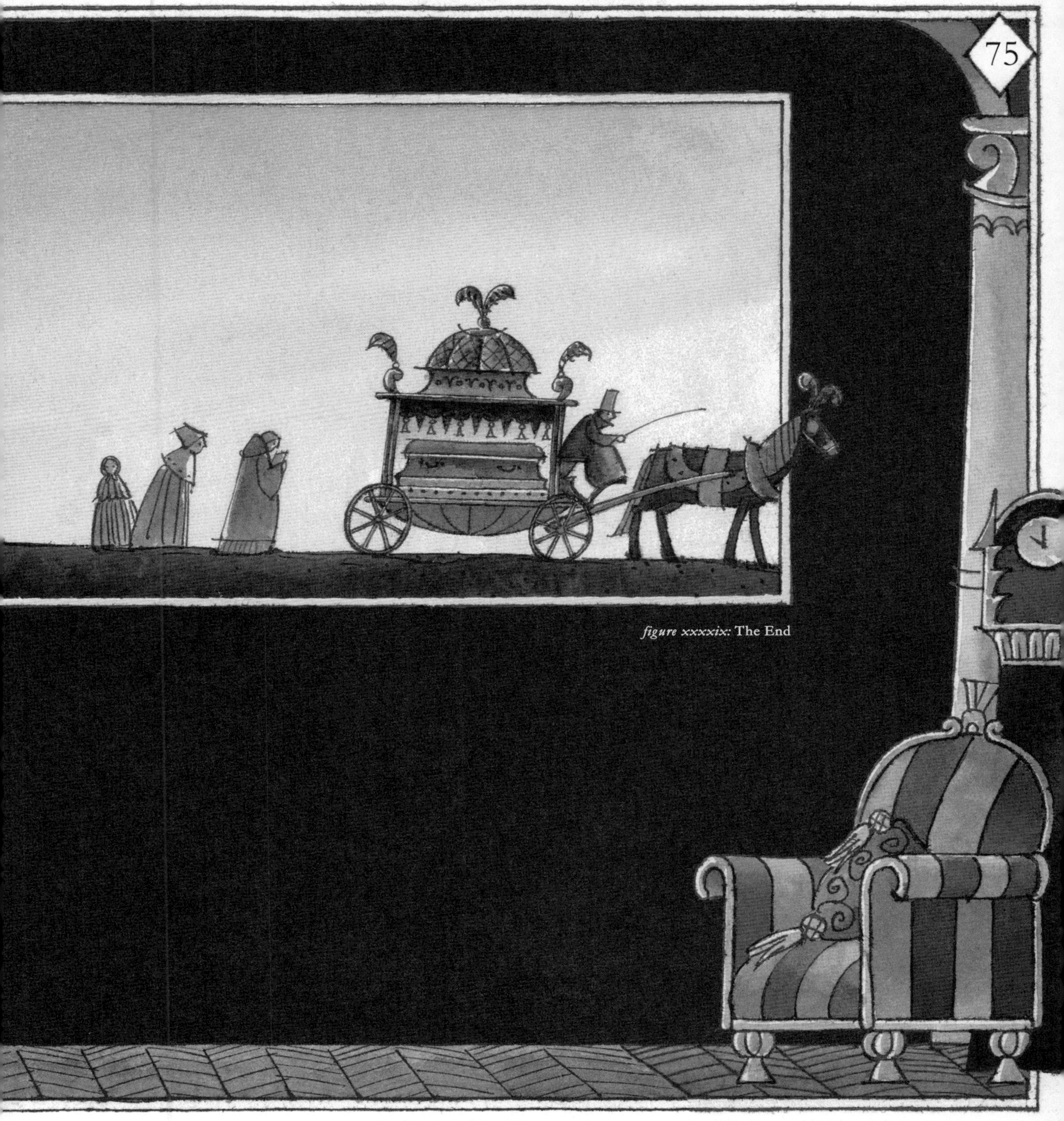

figure xxxxix: The End

The house was passed on in accordance with the old man's wishes
and became home to a big, boisterous family
and was filled with noise and voices.

But the youngest child was quiet and thoughtful
and often sat there in the chair in the Library, with a book on her lap,
looking across now and then at the empty plinth.

The story was that on the very day the little girl's great-uncle died,
the Statue, having sat there for centuries, quietly reading,
finished its book at last, got up and softly walked away.

And there on a high, high shelf, the little girl found the shut stone book.

And one day it fell open in her hands.

FAITH

figure xxxxx: behind the skirting board

A Death Watch Beetle tapped out a message
from behind the skirting board:
"It is a Lie that this dark and rotten world is all there is,
But the Truth is brighter than my poor eyes can bear."

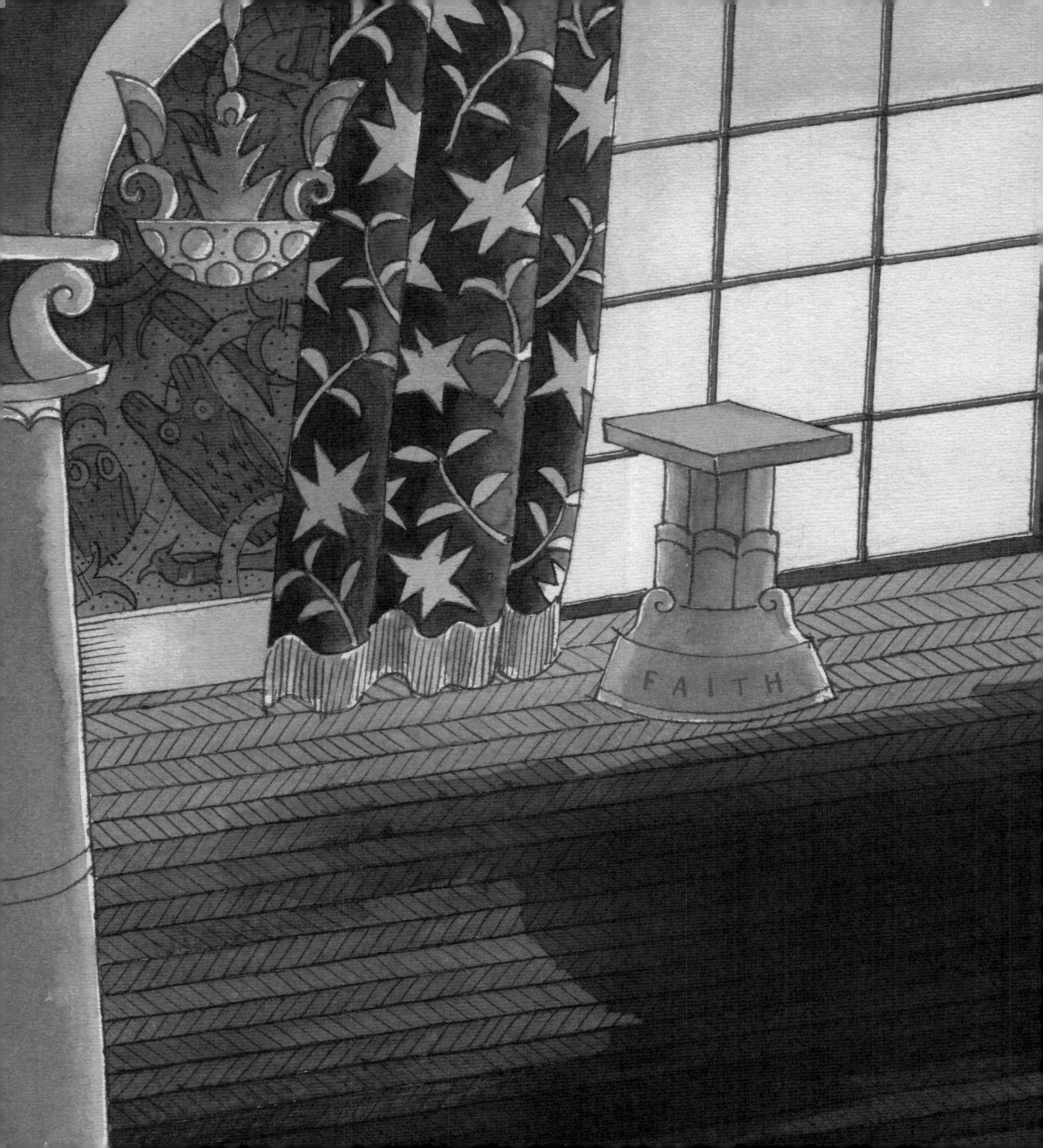
FAITH

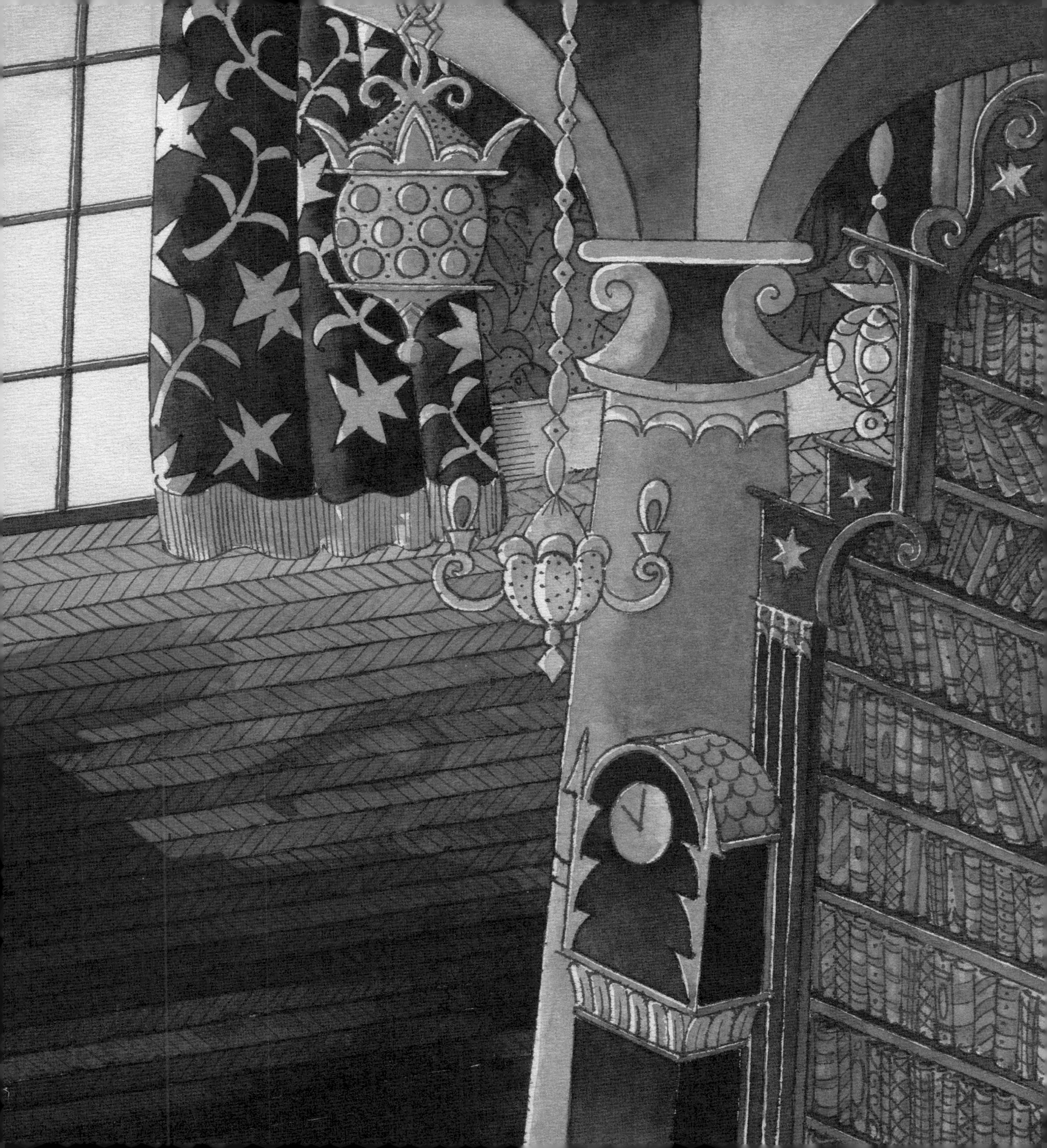

Other books by
DAVID LUCAS

Cake Girl
9781842706367

Halibut Jackson
9781842703717

Nutmeg
9781842705636

Whale
9781849391931

The Robot and the Bluebird
9781842707326